W0259481

OLD WORLD

BY THE SAME AUTHOR

POETRY

A Scottish Assembly
Sharawaggi (with W. N. Herbert)
Talkies
Masculinity
Spirit Machines
The Tip of My Tongue
Selected Poems
Apollos of the North
Full Volume
Simonides
Testament
The Scottish Ambassador

ANTHOLOGIES

Other Tongues: Young Scottish Poets in English, Scots and Gaelic (editor)
The Penguin Book of Poetry from Britain and Ireland since 1945 (with Simon Armitage)
The New Penguin Book of Scottish Verse (with Mick Imlah)
Scottish Religious Poetry (with Meg Bateman and James McGonigal)
The Book of St Andrews (editor)

NON-FICTION

The Savage and the City in the Work of T.S. Eliot
Devolving English Literature
Identifying Poets: Self and Territory in Twentieth-Century Poetry
The Modern Poet
Scotland's Books: The Penguin History of Scottish Literature
Robert Burns and Cultural Authority (editor)
The Scottish Invention of English Literature (editor)
Heaven-Taught Fergusson (editor)
Contemporary Poetry and Contemporary Science (editor)
The Bard: Robert Burns, A Biography
Bannockburns
Young Eliot: From St Louis to The Waste Land
Eliot After The Waste Land

OLD WORLD

Robert Crawford

CAPE POETRY

1 3 5 7 9 10 8 6 4 2

Jonathan Cape, an imprint of Vintage, is part of the Penguin Random House group
Vintage, Penguin Random House UK, One Embassy Gardens,
8 Viaduct Gardens, London SW11 7BW

First published in Great Britain by Jonathan Cape in 2025

penguin.co.uk/vintage
global.penguinrandomhouse.co.uk

Typeset in 11/13pt Bembo Book MT Pro by Jouve (UK), Milton Keynes
Printed and bound in Great Britain by TJ Books, Padstow, Cornwall

The authorised representative in the EEA is Penguin Random House Ireland, Morrison Chambers, 32 Nassau Street, Dublin D02 YH68

A CIP catalogue record for this book is available from the British Library

ISBN 9781787334564

Penguin Random House is committed to a sustainable future for our business, our readers and our planet. This book is made from Forest Stewardship Council® certified paper.

for Alice, Lewis, and Blyth
with love

The world is nothing
But a single drop of dew.
Nevertheless . . .

Issa

CONTENTS

DIVERSITY TRAINING

Starter

I have traced the source
Of spring through the hazel woods
To this single bud.

★

Summer

The bird climbs the sky
Without pitons, cords or ropes,
But not without song.

★

Infatuation

Impossible loves –
Too many to be counted –
Falling autumn leaves.

★

Tracker

Watch these snow-goose tracks
In snow, slowly vanishing
Below fresher snow.

OLD WORLD

Who can see the green earth any more
As she was by the sources of Time?
Who imagines her fields as they lay
In the sunshine, unworn by the plough?

Matthew Arnold, 'The Future'

Barley field, cut, dried,
Brewed, poured, you're so garrulous
Long after you've gone.

Old English Riddle from the *Exeter Book*

I

1

What rutting beast snorts
'Let me give you some pointers'
Then trots through the mist?

2

In the beginning
Was the Word, and the Word was
Parsed into creatures.

3

I am a hunter
Until the moment comes when
My quarry is milk.

4

My females are brown,
My males are black, though always
My song is pink, pink.

5

Seduced by AI,
We're already impatient
With a frail, old world.

6

We are baptised now
By our total immersion
In Loch Computer.

7

In a data trice
We glean the harvest that's kept
Ravelled inside light.

II

8

You get off my land
Up in the air as I heave
You out of the nest.

9

My elongation
Approaches its apogee
In legs, neck, and ears.

10

All soar and wingspan,
What idiot would want to
Hang me round their neck?

11

I gulp flies. I fly
South for the winter, darting,
Overtaking spring.

III

12

The one greatest gift
Is to fuse the riddle with
The riddle's answer.

13

We somehow lost touch.
How could we have forgotten
All our neighbours' names?

14

Our lives together
Are not easy, but they are
Our lives together.

15

You can lead a horse
To water, then patiently
Sit and watch it drink.

IV

16

Each morning, to wash,
I pack my trunk with water
Then hose myself down.

17

I lie wise in lochs,
But, having coursed through ocean,
I will jump for joy.

18

I eat another,
Then another colonist
Ad infinitum.

19

I relish the buzz,
The highs, but I relish most
That sting in my tail.

V

20

I am a sly, red
Machiavelli, barking
And stinking of heat.

21

To target cancer
Needs precise calibration
And a hinted kiss.

22

Haiku are pollen,
Bright angels danced off
The head of a pin.

23

I feather my nest
With dazzling embezzled coins
And worthless tinfoil.

24

The chuckie-skimmer's
Wrist-flick teaches us the art
Of letting things go.

VI

25

Hop light, hop light, off
I go, green as a soldier,
But always singing.

26

Wherever we are
We love the sand, earth, or sea
Which is almost ours.

27

Walking, not talking,
I turn up my nose at you
And am your best pal.

VII

28

Always time to flit:
Even when I'm upside down
My ears miss nothing.

29

Each ear of wheat hears.
You only have to listen
To each ear of wheat.

VIII

30

I eat anything
But am an unwanted guest
Whose gift is famines.

31

Lord, save us from jets
And smug, breathless SUVs
And meat; but not yet.

IX

32

A small island bird
Drops its shadow on the sand
Then dives to find it.

33

True eloquence is
The Down's Syndrome boy ringing
The old abbey bell.

X

34

Dogs run rings round us.
We rise damp, rank, and matted.
We need a good shave.

35

Exhibitionist,
Swinger, I fondle my tool
And look quite like you.

36

All through school and work
I clouded plate-glass windows
With my bated breath.

37

Knitting in summer –
Intricately odd, useless
Until winter comes.

XI

38

My game's playing dead.
I can't for the life of me
Think how to wake up.

39

The future was not
The Citroën Deux Chevaux.
It was two horses.

40

Bounce! Bounce! Bounce! Bounce! Bounce!
Hey – a manic depressive
With a baby on board.

41

Noah's saddest beast
Crossed continents, arriving
Alone at the ark.

XII

42

Wink to the mirror:
You have never looked better
Since a day ago.

43

Just like the ocean
The Large Hadron Collider
Flexes with the moon.

44

I'm saving myself
For a very long journey:
God gave me the hump.

45

Eternal start-up,
Organic light emitter,
Hallowed be thy name.

XIII

46

My pelt is Tipp-Ex.
I'm the tip of the iceberg.
I go with the floe.

47

In black and white prints
I'm just too photogenic,
Fellating bamboo.

48

Each day is a gift,
Though not quite, as it once was,
So freely given.

XIV

49

Greedy big shitter,
I fool you, following wakes
Of fishing boats home.

50

We learn from mirrors
That we are unknowable
Even to ourselves.

51

I move small mountains,
Travelling on a subway
Of my own design.

52

With bright, hair-fine wires
The earliest LEDs
Wove a nest of gold.

53

We want the wisdom
Caught fast in the uncluttered
Nonchalance of light.

XV

54

I am fleet of foot,
Carrying everywhere
These four lucky feet.

55

Main man, I'm the king.
In my pride I'm the show-off.
Pure dental. All mouth.

56

Each sunrise makes sure
The work of enlightenment
Continues unquenched.

XVI

57

God is both the word
And the white paper on which
The word is written.

58

Just for an instant
Liberté, égalité,
The freeing of light.

XVII

59

I sound like a toy,
But believe me, friend, this here's
No baby's rattle.

60

Do Wittgenstein's shrewd
'Family resemblances'
Make wild beasts our kin?

61

Leather, I lie flat,
Counting my teeth, and just may
See you, in a while.

XVIII

62

The moon teaches us
Weird originality
Would be a mistake.

63

What is it, honey,
Where is it, honey, oh, please
Lead me right to it.

64

'Art's origins lie
Deep in the old farming songs
Of seed-time.' (Bashō)

65

All day and all night
Without wool, wheel, or needles,
I'm an old weaver.

66

Serene and buoyant
Over Roshven's mountain range
Floats the harvest moon.

CAEDMON'S HYMN

from the Old English

Hymn Him who guards skies
For His grand design, His strong,
Long-established plan;

Eternal Maker,
Who started stars, Creator
Of heaven's high roof,

We give praise for when,
Last, as everlasting Lord,
You gave earth to men.

THE WEST LAND

A Global Warning

for Jahan Ramazani, il miglior critico

'Nam Sibyllam quidem Cumis ego ipse oculis meis vidi in ampulla pendere, et cum illi pueri dicerent: *Sibylla ti theleis*; respondebat illa: *Australia thelo.*'

I. *The Burrow of the Dead*

April is the crudest month, maxing
Out on air-lifted flowers, bleeding us dry, reheating
Memory's desires, stuffing and stiffing
Drought's tuberous roots once more in autumn's spring.
Winter in Oz is Europe's summer; Munich's winter
Perth (Western Australia)'s summer. Flesh and bone,
I listen to the Shadows and the Stones rock
Much of the night in this deserted burrow.
Thunder-dry beneath heaped desert sky
I will show you fear of fire in a land full of dust.

A crowd, Tiresias, flowed over Matagarup Bridge,
Infernal, heading for dead downtown towers,
O virtual city, hyacinth-gal Perth, *mon Acropole, mon coeur.*

II. *Game*

The chair she games in, burnished with putti, cracks,
Creaks, as she cries, her reinvented voice
At tea for two is a nightingale's *Eheu!* 'Oho!'
'How can you think about Western Australia
At a time like this?'
'I think we are all in Western Australia,
Doing nothing, while Earth burns
And we burn too. Burning is not a game.'

HURRY UP, HURRY UP PLEASE, IT'S 60 DEGREES, CALL 999!
Or else, sweet ladies of Perth, it is goodnight.

III. *The Fire Service*

O Swan (Derbarl Yerrigan) and Canning (Djarlgarra) Rivers
That surge through the West Land, then on through central Perth,
Flow gently, sweet Afton, till I end my song

And Mrs Margarate Porter, singing to her daughter,
As, surprised, they drown, hosed down by firemen, in rising water
Under the black smoke of a summer noon
Carthago delenda est
While I see the city of Perth burning, submerged, and giving birth
To red Carthage Sao Paolo Alexandria with its ruined books,
To a burning babe that connects net zero with nothing
Except this sweating globe of sands and fire

O my luve's like a red, red rose *wa wa*
red *red*

IV. *Deadly Water*

Forget the Phoenicians! Now it's climate refugees who queue
To be plucked from torrents of fire and floodwater too,
Water that has flooded Sydney suburbs, water that could drown
even you,
O Perth in the West Land, consider what you must do.

V. *What* The Thunderer *Said*

After the old boys in London pubs and clubs,
After China and India peer through their monsoon smog,
And America and Egypt and Russia cough in the fog,
The fucked-up fug,
Then the *Times* reports no water, only rock
And dry sand in Western Australia's deserts beyond Perth.
This is the re-sung song of burning and scorched earth.
MA
M.A.: Not all the M.A.s from Harvard and Glasgow and Sheffield
and Waseda will save us
Nor all the B.Sc.s and PhDs
Till we are on our knees
MA
Mannahatta: Pray in Mannahatta's MOMA and in Boston, Mass., O
makars, pray
For coolness – not the slick
Coolness of the selfie click
Like the click of a key in a lock
With the clock's tick-tock TikTok talk talk talk –
But the coolness of cool Siloam's shady rill
Where, dear heart, you can drink your fill
Of that cooling water,
O far Fair Maid of Perth,
MA

Mamma mamma: O mothers and daughters of the world unite
In an urgent pageant
To show
What all must do and where we all must go

O lux perpetua

Matagarup Bridge is falling down falling down falling down

Timor mortis conturbat me
I hear full-fathom-five voices on the radio say
O Ganges brinkman-ship O life boat O hollow hollow
Qu'a ce reffrain ne vous remaine:
Mais ou sont les neiges d'antan?
M.A. Mannahatta. Mamma mamma.
O ship of singing fools'

Shanties shanties shanties

RULER

Mesour is tresour

(John Lydgate, citing a medieval proverb)

1

I aim to measure
The entire planet, using
This haiku ruler.

Estimated number of surviving yellow-billed loons: 20,000.

2

I come in packs, packed
With plague, and I'll betray you
Just by a whisker.

Estimated number of surviving mountain gorillas: 540.

3

Man is the measure
And measurer of all things,
So we used to think.

Estimated number of surviving night parrots: 200.

4

The Decline and Fall
Of the Roman Empire is
My magnum opus.

Estimated number of surviving giant ibises: 345.

5

Coronavirus
Edits all inessentials
And leaves us birdsong.

Estimated number of surviving forest bitterns: 5000.

6

My organ donors
Too numerous to mention,
I have earned my stripes.

Estimated number of surviving marine otters: 1000.

7

Hand-writing the words
Soon I shall cease to exist
Is life-affirming.

Estimated number of surviving blue-throated macaws: 130.

8

A poet says I
Stare at nothing with one eye
And then pick it up.

Estimated number of surviving komodo dragons: 4000.

9

Misunderstanding
Is part of each age, as in
Edvard Munch's *The Sneeze.*

Estimated number of surviving Bengal tigers: 2917.

10

I am that filly
No one has ever ridden.
I dance, curly-tailed.

Estimated number of surviving glow-throated hummingbirds: 700.

11

The dark central hole
Adds value to the single
Norwegian crown coin.

Estimated number of surviving common wombats 7000.

12

Tell it slant. Sideways
Is best, or so I maintain,
As I scuttle on.

Estimated number of surviving Siberian tigers: 540.

HUNGER

I picked a bayberry
I picked a dayberry
I picked a burberry
I picked a breadberry
I picked a chokeberry
I picked a baneberry
I picked a wineberry
I picked a oneberry
I picked a Juneberry
I picked a youngberry
I picked a bogberry
I picked a dogberry
I picked a hackberry
I picked a blackberry
I picked an inkberry
I picked a pinkberry
I picked a bilberry
I picked a mulberry
I picked a cranberry
I picked a snowberry
I picked a crowberry
I picked a strawberry
I picked a squawberry
I picked a barberry
I picked a deerberry
I picked a mossberry
I picked a raspberry
I picked a catberry
I picked a dewberry
I picked a blueberry
I picked a gooseberry
And that was the last

OLD ENGLISH HAIKU

Four riddles from the Exeter Book

Ship's Figurehead

Girl, one-off, grey crone,
I flew with birds, dived, landed,
And once had a soul.

Iceberg

On the ocean waves
A wonderful thing: water
Scrimshawed, become bone.

Book

Bald, lined, bent double
And bound to serve, I'll teach you
All you need to know.

Book-worm

Weird, digesting books,
Gobbling epics, no wiser
For taking in words.

MEXICAN HAIKU LIVES

Peacock

De haut en bas bird,
You cross democracy's coop
Like a procession.

Toads

Penumbral mud-pies
Littering the avenue
Just blast off and jump.

Flying Fish

Smacked by solar gold,
The wide ocean's windowpanes
Splinter into shards.

Willow

Gentle pensioner,
Almost gold, almost amber,
Almost pure sunlight.

after José Juan
Tablada, Mexico's grand
Master haikuist

FOUR JAPANESE CRIES

Over a dark sea
The piping of the teal brings
Dim, distant whiteness.

★

Carrying for miles,
The cuckoo's insistent call
Crosses the water.

★

A flash of lightning
At the onset of darkness
Is the heron's cry.

★

Out of still silence,
Rasping deep into the rocks
A cicada's song.

after Bashō

TREE

lines from the Old English 'Dream of the Rood'

Now! Hear how I dreamed a great dream
Way after midnight while most men slept.
I seemed to see the tree of glory
Held high in heaven, haloed with light,
A blazing beacon, gleaming with jewels,
Five stars – strong candles – arrayed as a cross.
A sky full of angels eyed it with awe;
But through gold's glint I still could glimpse
Sure signs of torture, as those sacred branches
Suddenly started to speak:

'Years, years ago, I remember it yet,
They chopped me down at a copse's edge,
Logged, uprooted me. Devils removed me,
Jackals made me a jailbirds' gibbet.
Foemen shouldered me, forced and hewed me,
Shifted me, set me up, stood on a hill
Till I looked on the Lord, that Man of mankind,
In his hero's hurry to climb my high beams.
Then I dared not go against God's word,
Bow down nor break. I had to stand
When the young hero, High King of Heaven,
Strong, stout-hearted, started to climb me
Clear in his mission to redeem mankind.
When he touched me, I flinched, but feared to fall

Slumped to the soil. *I had to stand,*
Created a cross, *to carry that King*
The stars' strong Lord. *I had to stand*
As they drove in dark nails; *deep, cruel wounds,*

Still scar me, unhealed. *I could not staunch them.*
They cursed us both *as, blackened with blood*
Shed from his side, *I stood as creation wept.*
Dark clouds slewed over. *I had to stand*
Far from that copse *at the forest's edge,*
Hacked, nail-battered tree, *I had to stand,*
Crying for the killed King, *Christ on his cross.'*

THEOLOGY

God is our word for
Being attuned to the thrum
Of the universe.

God is manifest
In giant sequoias most
When they are still seeds.

God is the old nag
Who nagged and nagged us before
The world was burning.

God is where I put
All that will never be known
When my dust settles.

Our visions of God
Are forever lopsided
Like a one-eared hare.

OBSOLETE BROKEN ANGEL

Old
Cold
Plaster-cast
Of a masterpiece,
Thin,
One-winged
Amputee from mid-air,
Cast aside
In the powder-dry
Museum store,
Half-healed,
Hallowed with damage,
Haloed
With a ring
Of pain,
Again and again,
Apparently worth
Nothing
You express
Through your silent cry
To the damaged Earth
So much more
Because broken
Than you could express
Intact,
Your cracked,
Unsteady
Body,
Your one
Outstretched hand's third
Finger gone,
Almost lost
Signpost,

Gaunt perch
For the descent
Or ascent
Of a phosphorus-bright,
Healing
White
Bird.

GRIDS

AI's grid poems
Can be published, scaled up, as
Drone murmurations.

CONTACT LESS CONTACT LESS CONTACT LESS
CONTACT LESS CONTACT LESS CONTACT LESS
CONTACT LESS CONTACT LESS CONTACT LESS
CONTACT LESS CONTACT LESS CONTACT LESS
CONTACT LESS CONTACT LESS CONTACT LESS
CONTACT LESS CONTACT LESS CONTACT LESS
CONTACT LESS CONTACT LESS CONTACT LESS
CONTACT LESS CONTACT LESS CONTACT LESS
CONTACT LESS CONTACT LESS CONTACT LESS
CONTACT LESS CONTACT LESS CONTACT LESS
CONTACT LESS CONTACT LESS CONTACT LESS
CONTACT LESS CONTACT LESS CONTACT LESS
CONTACT LESS CONTACT LESS CONTACT LESS
CONTACT LESS CONTACT LESS CONTACT LESS
CONTACT LESS CONTACT LESS CONTACT LESS
CONTACT LESS CONTACT LESS CONTACT LESS
CONTACT LESS CONTACT LESS CONTACT LESS
CONTACT LESS CONTACT LESS CONTACT LESS
CONTACT LESS CONTACT LESS CONTACT LESS
CONTACT LESS CONTACT LESS CONTACT LESS

The forest hermits
Can no more leave the forest
Than the trees themselves.

WIFIWIFEWIFIWIFEWIFIWIFEWIFIWIFE
WIFIWIFEWIFIWIFEWIFIWIFEWIFIWIFE
WIFIWIFEWIFIWIFEWIFIWIFEWIFIWIFE
WIFIWIFEWIFIWIFEWIFIWIFEWIFIWIFE
WIFIWIFEWIFIWIFEWIFIWIFEWIFIWIFE
WIFIWIFEWIFIWIFEWIFIWIFEWIFIWIFE
WIFIWIFEWIFIWIFEWIFIWIFEWIFIWIFE
WIFIWIFEWIFIWIFEWIFIWIFEWIFIWIFE
WIFIWIFEWIFIWIFEWIFIWIFEWIFIWIFE
WIFIWIFEWIFIWIFEWIFIWIFEWIFIWIFE
WIFIWIFEWIFIWIFEWIFIWIFEWIFIWIFE
WIFIWIFEWIFIWIFEWIFIWIFEWIFIWIFE
WIFIWIFEWIFIWIFEWIFIWIFEWIFIWIFE
WIFIWIFEWIFIWIFEWIFIWIFEWIFIWIFE
WIFIWIFEWIFIWIFEWIFIWIFEWIFIWIFE
WIFIWIFEWIFIWIFEWIFIWIFEWIFIWIFE

Just like those dazzled
Natives who met Columbus
We have no new world.

INBOXINBOXINBOXINBOXINBOXINBOXIN
INBOXINBOXINBOXINBOXINBOXINBOXIN
INBOXINBOXINBOXINBOXINBOXINBOXIN
INBOXINBOXINBOXINBOXINBOXINBOXIN
INBOXINBOXINBOXINBOXINBOXINBOXIN
INBOXINBOXINBOXINBOXINBOXINBOXIN
INBOXINBOXINBOXINBOXINBOXINBOXIN
INBOXINBOXINBOXINBOXINBOXINBOXIN
INBOXINBOXINBOXINBOXINBOXINBOXIN
INBOXINBOXINBOXINBOXINBOXINBOXIN
INBOXINBOXINBOXINBOXINBOXINBOXIN
INBOXINBOXINBOXINBOXINBOXINBOXIN
INBOXINBOXINBOXINBOXINBOXINBOXIN
INBOXINBOXINBOXINBOXINBOXINBOXIN
INBOXINBOXINBOXINBOXINBOXINBOXIN
INBOXINBOXINBOXINBOXINBOXINBOXIN
INBOXINBOXINBOXINBOXINBOXINBOXIN

OLD WORLD EMBLEMS

The old world's old words
Are emblems of the living
And of the unborn.

I re-hang my sign
BACK UNDER OLD MANAGEMENT
As I start again.

Y P

S H

I V

S S

Underestimate
At your own risk, world, the harsh
Selfishness of fire.

PRO ME THE VS

Persisting, I show
How being a woman now
Is a world-wide web.

P

O E

L N

E

Our artificial
Intelligence must become
A queer kind of love.

G A I A

I'm always making
A spectacle of myself
As you can still see.

gOrgOn

In each partnership
There's a stubborn imbalance
That never changes.

ROMVLVS

& REMVS

To see things my way's
Challenging, but I suffer
From high self-esteem.

I

CYCLOPS

Pushing the boat out
Runs in my veins: *thus far, then*
Just a bit further.

R
V
B
I
C
O
N

Still texted more than
All other classical texts,
I'm the odd one out.

CORONA

V

IR

VS

There is always more
Than we're able to cope with
Except in our dreams.

V
TANTAL S

There comes a time when
All you'll get out of me is
No more to be said.

ceNsOr

THREE SCOTTISH MINIATURES

I have kept in-house
My removal company,
Though work remains slow.

★

I add and add and
I add and add and add and
Then I add and add.

★

Glowing on sonar,
Whole shoals of us, scaled up, each
A silver darling.

VOAR

Whaur's the hame-comin o voar?
Aa burd-alane; nae gate.
If aabody kens jist whaur
Voar gangs, caa it tae wait.

Voar laves nae smitch. Wha kens?
But speir o thae yalla burds.
Flichtin owre breers in the wund
A hunner sangs' haithen wurds.

SPRING

Where is the return of spring? All completely alone; no road. If anyone knows just where spring goes, call it to occur. Spring leaves no trace. Who knows? But ask those yellow birds. Fluttering over wild roses in the wind – a hundred songs' incomprehensible words.

after the Chinese of Huang Tingjian

SCREIVIT WHILL FOU IN THE HOOSE ABUNE THE LOCH

Banff baillies come but dinnae dern yon ben.
Beguess the baits are boordit by the drift.
The yird is soopit by a blash o wun.
I jist tak tent o the loch glessin the lift.

WRITTEN WHILE DRUNK IN THE HOUSE ABOVE THE LAKE

Big storm clouds come but do not hide that mountain. Randomly the boats are boarded by the snow. The earth is swept by a sudden blast of wind. I only notice the lake mirroring the sky.

after the Chinese of Su Dongpo

THINKIN O GANGIN OOT ON A WEET DAY

Black weet blaws frae the aist,
Fashin yon traivellers.
The causey that was stour
Is noo aa glaur.

Flooirs an sauchs snoozle.
Spring is aa a sloonge,
An me, ach weel, een mair nor spring
I'm a sloonge tae.

THINKING OF GOING OUTSIDE ON A RAINY DAY

Heavy rain blows from the east, annoying those travellers. The roadway that was dust is now all mud. Flowers and willow trees doze. Spring is a total layabout, and I, oh well, even more than spring, I'm a layabout too.

after the Chinese of Lu Yu

LOCKDOWN

1

Each one of us, perched
On the skerry of our self,
Must build a lighthouse.

2

The rock is almost
As we long for it to be,
Inaccessible.

3

One beacon demands
Huge, hard-won keystones, stalwart
Stanchions of iron.

4

We haul granite blocks
With a derrick and tackle
To raise high the walls.

5

The dead of neap-tide's
Absolute emptiness makes
The best time to work.

6

We can build only
In the short summer season
Before big storms hit.

7

Each gale or flood-tide
Threatens to obliterate
All we've accomplished.

8

In our lighthouses
Each of us hides, reaching out
To a life beyond.

9

And when the work's done
The light's not to lure others
But to warn them off.

SMALL BULK

The hemlock vial
Does the job much better than
The jeroboam.

IN MEMORY OF CYNTHIA STALLMAN-PACITTI

Blue-cagouled, nimble raconteuse,
Byzantinist with a laugh like a bomb,

Last seen on Iona, you left the party
Early, at the age of thirty-six.

I remember the gleaming crown
Held above you at your Orthodox wedding,

And your joke about an old narcoleptic soprano
Who nodded off, but was held in place

By her loyal choir as she toppled forwards
In the middle of the twenty-third psalm.

PALM TREE

after Abd al-Rahman

in memory of Maria Rosa Menocal

Dead-centre at Rusafa, in the loam,
This palm was seeded as a refugee.
'You know me, I know you, old, exiled tree:
We each will die at home here, far from home.'

FACTS ABOUT R.C.

He was born and baptised in Xi'an, Shaanxi.
His uncle, aunt, and their ten-month-old son were publicly beheaded.
He lived in a fifteenth-century tower-house.
His second language was English, Mandarin his first.
He edited a book called *Restoring Scotland's Castles*.
He did not go to university.
He spent four days, aged eight, stowed in a cargo-ship hold with no toilet.
He was interned as a child for five years by the Japanese in Weihsien.
He ran the world's oldest continuously trading bookshop.
He suffered from dementia, fell, and broke his hip.
He was rescued by Hershey's chocolate-bearing American troops.
He wrote in a notepad what his workers took in their tea and coffee, then made it.
He attended boarding school when his parents returned as missionaries to China.
He was shipped from Asia to Southampton wearing a tag reading 'R. Clow, Hong Kong.'
His guardian was a man called J. Knox.
He changed his starched shirt-collar twice a day in smoky Glasgow.
He enjoyed playing bridge.
He saved the River Clyde from becoming a bus station.
He was reserved and loved fun.
He hardly ever spoke about being a prisoner of the Japanese.
He was trained as a bookseller by an acquaintance of Dame Edith Sitwell.
He helped rescue St Vincent Terrace.
His shop traded under the name of John Smith and Son.
He married Katrina, a botanist.
His bookshop had its own six-berth yacht and a medieval French chateau for staff use.
He owned 95 acres of farmland and woods.

His now defunct shop's emblem is carved on a building in Market
Street, St Andrews.
His shop sold me Donne, Spenser, Dryden, Pope, Wordsworth,
Hardy, Eliot, Auden, Muir.
His shop sold me Bartok, Beethoven, Brahms, Bruckner, Chopin,
Elgar, De Falla, Mahler.
He opened doors.
'He didn't do this for show. It was just him.'

Robert Clow, Glasgow bookseller (1934–2022)

ROGER LONSDALE

Obituarist needed. Email the city of Hull:
A wry son has fallen. Carry word north beyond Yorkshire:
Alert Barter Books. Light beacons on Eglingham moor
And along Alnmouth beach where he flew as a navigator
On National Service. Notify London.
Divert Dr Burney from his harpsichord
To break the drab news. Inform Dr Johnson's teapot.
Ring Yale and Oxford. Hunt Holywell Street high and low.
Comb the Music Room. Description: Englishman, pipe-cleaner-thin,
In an ever-grey suit, furtively smoking, amused
By the Scots at Balliol, still loyal only to Bruce. Yell to Devorgilla.
Buzz the Snell Bridge. Wake up those show-offy dons.
Tell Gray, Collins, and Goldsmith. Whisper to the buttery staff
Who knew his tipple, to the staff of stacked Thornton's bookshop
Where once he popped in and bought Burns's *Poems* with a poem
By Burns in manuscript inside. Let the board of Blackwell's wear black
And the OUP shop in the High close forever in tribute.
Tell tubby Ted Heath; tell tottery Harold Macmillan;
Tell Hooray Henry Boris and Hooray Henrietta Ghislaine;
Tell all the (im)moral tutees; and take word, too,
To Roy Park on the Quinag, to Fiona Stafford, to Nick Hudson out
in Vancouver,
To Lady Mary Wortley Montagu, Anonymous, and Mehetabel Wright.
Tell all the male poets whose *Lives* he helped sort out
And all the women poets he added in nudge after nudge.
Tell Inspector Morse and Sergeant Lewis to tear round
To Lonsdale College, but arrive too late.
Dislodge the Master from the Master's Lodgings
To speak blandly and raise a glass.
Tell the British Academy to wail and update its website.
Comfort shareholders in tobacco companies. They will feel this loss.
They'll never hear the like of his dry cough again.
Put rare-book dealers on standby. Start them salivating.

But now because one sunny afternoon I saw him almost weep
In Manor Walk; because at High Table
He assured me it was alright not to feel at home,
Take news of him to Dick Ellmann heading home in his Saab
And to Marilyn and David Butler giving my parents a lift in their
    Mini Metro,
So they can tell all the dead, as I tell the living,
Something of this man whose Wikipedia entry
Is just two lines long, his errors 'not indecently numerous'.
Slow the traffic to ode-speed on the Woodstock and Banbury Roads.
Back-up tour buses beside Balliol's side-wall. Tell them
So the story may spread, even if all that's remembered
Is a shadow, a wave, a quick word. Who can tell?

TANK

Age: 22. Time: after 2. Rumbling
On western skyline, barrage, tangled tracks, trucks,
Jeeps, flags, signposts, dust, oily rags, lorries tumbling
Over dark crests, pulverised surface almost liquid, like sticky,
Gritty faeces. Men knee-deep in it, goggled faces
Lost under thick, off-white masks, swigging from hip-flasks.

animula blandula vagula

Inside a wide, bucking two-ton, we're thrown
Against our own cab's sides and roof. All round, drab vehicles,
Winches, twenty-five-pounders, big guns grounded in pits,
Stench of petrol fires for brewing up tea, tinned meat knifed into bits.

Parched, in shirt and shorts, among parking
Tanks and trucks jumbled together, I blether, marking
Places on this cellophane mapcase with a chinagraph pencil,
And eye faces – one red with half-dead dry skin
Cracking on lips and nose; flannel shirt, ripped trousers, done-in
Shoes, blue-check handkerchief twisted round bruised neck;
Our rations new tins of beef, two
Of white potatoes, bright
Spick-and-span tins of canned bacon rashers,
Pocked fruit, condensed milk. Pair of clean socks: right
Stuffed with tea; left with rough, coarse sugar.

Also: small, dirty, ragged-handled bag with shirts,
Washing and shaving kit, bits of camera,
Paperback book; rolled in old valise and bedding:
Battledress and revolver; mask; writing paper;
Hidden in secret pocket girl's locket and small silver flask
Of whisky. Ration box stashed in half-smashed, nearly fried

Locker way back deep in the stinking tank
(Six-pounder gun, new three-man crew) – five wheels each side.

animula blandula vagula

Still guzzling veg stew swilled down with black-brown fresh-brewed coffee, we catch
Distant desultory thumps, jumpy bushes of fine dust smoking on the skyline, and watch
Planes high in blue, dry air, then hear devil-may-care shouts, whistled dance tunes,
Metallic clangs, bangs, long, long seconds of machine-gun sputter.
Quit now of HQ's bullshit,
As tank commander my rank means my place is right
Of the dark-muzzled six-pounder, peering through the stark periscope:
Very small view; in action with the crew, to see more
While the engine roars, I stand on the floor
Of that squat, angular, hot, dust-blown turret, eyes
Just clear of its top, or sit in the turret-top manhole, legs lolling down inside.
Behind each tank's barrel's breech a metal shield
Protects crews against the strong, foot-long recoil. Nearby's
A rack for the machine-gun's ammo stack, plus
Two choking smoke-dischargers, large six-pounder shells (nose down),
Hand- and smoke-grenades; jet-black map case; the radio set
Fixed at the turret's back has a control box to get
Switched from A set to internal comms, ready for ops; on top
Of the old radio set sit binoculars, spare parts, bits
Of machine-gun and magazines. Bored, we hoard books,
Boiled sweets, sheets of paper, processed cheese,
Butter, water, knives. We dream of wives and canned peas.

animula blandula vagula

The night stars are jewels on black velvet; starshells
Firework all over. So, too, do tracers'
Orange, green, red, blue, and starch-harsh white.
At 4am we're shaken awake. By 5, it's no longer night.
Tanks crouch like toads; engines are warmed. Rank, blue smoke
Burns with stagnant oil. Our tanks turn, avoiding ramming
One another in half-dark. From each stark turret
Come clear but bodiless voices. You hear
Hoarse operators curse through a din of Morse and jamming.

7am:
Tanks move off; men chew bacon, brew up
Hot tea in petrol tins with thin wire handles;
Bite into light oatcakes fried in bacon fat;
Oleomargarine. I spot a fat rat.
Rest of the single-file tank column's heading west: just
Turrets and pennants, blowing on small aerials showing above
billowing dust.

Afternoon: gunners jump to thump sporadic fire
Up at a silver plane, serenely high in blue sky
Among pudgy, smudged smoke-stains –
Its whistling bombs oddly lovely: a shower of rain's
Glittering, glistening droplets. I shout,
'Try to listen!' The tank engine's
Rise-fall revving drowns all other sounds –
The outside world glides slyly by like a silent film,
The Cabinet of Doctor Caligari.

Batches of 200 tired prisoners; patches on battledresses;
Burnt-out shell of enemy tank; a big Brueghel hell
Of vehicles burning on the cracked horizon, shrouds
Of black smoke thrown across orange sky. Light ebbs. Webs

Of shell traces arc over madly parked derelicts. A shitty smell
Comes from slit trenches in stony ground dug by thug-faced troops.

animula blandula vagula

Big bangs. Incoming mortar fire. Clangs on the turret.
Horus's sly eye painted on a manky tank
In sump oil and rank,
Foul-smelling black, maybe off dumped, stewed brew-tins.

'Be glad when this is over too, won't you, sir?' Exchange of banalities
Cheers us up. Mad barrage from lads on twenty-five pounders.
Counter-fire whistling, chattering, clattering,
Rumbling like trains, as if the whole ground's
Shaking. Next, mumblings and sounds
Of gasping, microphone-whispering, rasping tearing of cloth.
Snipers' bullets whine like tiny, innocuous insects.
After 4am-till-dawn duty, still
Keeping binoculars sweeping a distant hill.
The frisky Colonel's suede boots and low-grade pomade. Whisky.
'Oh, I suppose we've sunk pretty low, taking it for breakfast.'

6 a.m. Manoeuvres in bad light. Contact lost overnight.
Lonely. Only our third time in action as a unit.
Floundering over slit trenches. Another civilian hit,
Crushed, snapped by tank-tracks. We swerve around that booby-
   trapped wreck,
Covered with bedding and kit, near it a derelict half-track,
Then, between two bulky burnt-out hulks, slewed, 50 yards apart,
A smashed car. Incoming shells from far guns. Men dart
Behind dire, slashed bedding strapped to a tank still on fire.
Sulky silence. Fleas. Biscuits. Slivers of cheese.

The dark blue, steel-jacketed machine gun jams. A hatch slams.
   'What? What?'

'Can't hear you through these fucking earphones.' 'Going
To run back to stores for lemonade and buns.'
Dead soldier sprawled in a pit. A fly
Crawls over the dry pupil of his blank, unblinking right eye.

animula blandula vagula

Drained, glum prisoners crane their necks. Weapon pits
Swarm with toppled stacks of looted rifles, black pistols,
Eight pairs of lightweight binoculars, flat
Round tins of thin-cut enemy chocolate. After a sudden rat-a-tat,
High explosives land. The tanned, frisky Colonel
Wants gobbets of glory. Gaunt microphone and headphone flexes
Tangle up, shell cases littering the oddly-angled tank-turret's floor.

Twelve enemy tanks advance. Shots. Hot sparks
Fall all round us. Petrol lorries hit. Not enough cover.
Troops come out of the setting sun. Calls for smoke. Rout. Tanks
Reversing, milling around a killing-ground. 'Open fire. Range one zero zero zero.
Make each shot count. Give the bastards every round you've got. Over.'
The deflector bag fills, pell-mell, with empty shell cases, the turret clogs with smoke.

Twilight shifts to near-darkness. Cramped hell of fear and yells.
Shells tilting towards us, vanishing. Acrid smells.
Petrol lorries still blazing like beacons. Dead boys and wounded men.
After that, amazing sleep from 4 until 10 a.m.

animula blandula vagula

For forty-eight hours clanging gangs of fitters,
Lacerating fingers, use all their might
To remove the recalcitrant, close-fitting, tight

Mudguard from our scarred tank, stripping out forty yards
Of rusty spikes and coils of oily wire wound
Round the sprocket between the tank's wide track and side. More
Lacerations grow into yet more hard-to-heal sores.

Trying to rally us: 'Yea, though I walk through the valley of the
shadow of death . . .'
Missing faces. Perfectly done-up laces
Of the Colonel's suede boots
In tight reef-knots. Stray shots. At first light, the second phase.
Tonight, regrouped grim-faced troops
Are sent to attack. Planned-for casualties: 100%.

Stripping off the cardboard, ripping it from brass shells
With wasp-coloured noses, tearing rags and flags
From ammunition tins, priming grenades, checking bags,
Back-bins and lockers. Loosening ammunition in the racks.
Humphing God-knows-what in innumerable sacks.
Tank drivers wrench forever at fan belts with spanners,
Levering, fretting, sweating to tighten the tracks;
Inside, making nearly wrecked engines roar, they get gauges checked.
Five new tanks arrive, needing petrol, oil, water,
No bivouac tents strapped to their dented sides.
Whiny newbie loses tiny photograph of his daughter.
Racks need tightening – they lack some guns –
Other automatics half-hidden in a paste of waste oil and dirt.

Confusion. Jeep hit and driven into slit trench. Men laden
With bins of radio parts, tins of cheese, but no beef.
Grind along powdery tracks. Rifle cracks. Last of the night air. Dust.

One boy finds a gap in barbed-wire walls, crawls through a
minefield.
Line of our trucks blown up by our own gunners.

Corpses together in a pit. Blather. Foul, inky smoke. Lost runners.
Over-sized corpse seems to move, covered in towels.

'Get us out of here?' Trapped, blood-smeared infantrymen,
Faces twisted, hit in several places below knees.
Lying for days, no water. Crazed. Longing for release.
Got them on the tank. Drank hot coffee.

Our tanks still thrown by wire and prone to oil-leaks.
'Hup, hup! Disperse a bit, will you?' Shaken up. Reek of shit.
Inside the turret: deflector bag, radio, green rag, machine gun
And shells in rack splashed thick with blood; weird smells;
More shells on floor in inch-deep blood pool.
'Sorry. Bit mucky in the turret.'

animula blandula vagula

Scrape shallow trench beside tank. Sleep through stench,
  fully-dressed,
Rolled in blankets and old coat with torn picture of naked breast.
Parabolas of machine-gun bullets climb on, one by one, towards Orion.

Take another quick shit. Thick bodies of conscript infantrymen in
  weapon pit
With picture postcards: monochrome villages, family-at-home
  snapshots,
Chocolate wrappings, heap of cheap cigarette packets. Terrible cough.
Gap-toothed grin through yellow, carious teeth. Seen from the jeep:
Little tin 'red devil' grenades, and helmets, badges torn off.

Avoid big, scabby, booby-trapped body,
Each dead, peg-like leg broken at the knee.

animula blandula vagula

'Oh shit! My fucking trousers won't fit!' 'They sharp tin buttons
Start bloody cutting themselves off, son,
Soon as they get bloody sewn on.'
Radio gives out. Shout instructions, cloaked in smoke bombs.
Earsplitting bursts of HE. Three copies of a glossy mag
Glimpsed in muck, blood and oil stains on spoiled tuxedos.

Jump from the tank: trousers fall down below rump.
Bashing holes in petrol cans with Stan's looted bayonet.
Amazing brew on, but need a piss. Blazing tank approaching,
Red aureole around its turret top, not-yet-dead driver's mop-headed
  white face black.
Fire-extinguishers hissing and missing.

Our twenty-five-pounders, off calibration, drop rounds
Randomly amongst us. 'Fuck! Fuck! Fuck! Fuck! Fuck!'
Hole in dead adjutant's head. Gutted truck.

Westwards again, past line of tired men and telegraph poles,
Downed plane's tail sticking upwards, a tiny, frail arrow in the earth.

Twelve enemy tanks, out of range,
But now, suddenly, approaching fast – strange,
Shapeless and blurred through a tough belt of slurred smoky haze.
Mistaken for trees. Fired on. They freeze, then accelerate away.

Ready to move. Dead Major. Men fled.
We machine-gun lorry engines. Near the railway, more trucks, but,
  luckily, road clear.
Name of station written on a thin tin plate.
Spoils. A first-aid find: scissors, instruments, lined
Notepad, ink erasers, high-necked jersey, badges, combs, razors,

Hair-cream. 'They're surrendering!' A scream. Twenty-seven tanks, some ablaze.
Inside one, the crew's wan bodies blasted round the turret's walls.

animula blandula vagula

When our tank's blown up by a great booby-trapped crate, the men
Hitch back, perched on another tank. Airfield evacuated. Faces numb and blank.

Downpour. Soaked floor. Landing-ground turns to marsh.
Dank clothes dry out later, draped round tank's exhaust.
Dejected, hodden-grey-faced prisoners given sodden pieces of biscuit.
Line of charred, abandoned vehicles near minefield. Hard-
Eyed captured sarge with half-fried book, *Also sprach Zarathustra*.
Major cries: 'No fraternising. They will only despise you.'
Next morning, sniper finds him. No warning. Too late.
Need sleep. Need eyes tested: cracked lens. Got to see straight.

after Keith Douglas

This poem, made during battles in Europe in 2022, reworks passages from the first half of the prose memoir Alamein to Zem Zem *(Editions Poetry London, 1946) by Keith Douglas (1920–44). Early in that memoir Douglas misquotes from memory the first words – 'Animula vagula, blandula [Little life, charming and wandering]' – from the Roman Emperor Hadrian's deathbed poem saying farewell to his soul.*

ELECTRONIC TEXT CORPUS OF SUMERIAN LITERATURE: PROVERBS

Ye dinnae speik anent
Aa ye've git, ye speik anely
Anent aa ye've tint.

You do not speak about
All you've found, you speak only
About all you've lost.

★

Offert, haun raxes
Oot tae haun, a haun aipens
Fur an aipened haun.

Offered, hand reaches
Out to hand, a hand opens
For an opened hand.

★

Dugs tell their maisters
'If ye carena fur pleisure
Ye'll nae miss oor lack.'

Dogs tell their masters
'If you care not for pleasure
You'll not miss our loss.'

★

In ben the pailace:
Ae day a mither gies birth;
Neist, a mither greets.

Inside the palace:
One day a mother gives birth;
Next, a mother weeps.

★

The swipper yin hid;
The strang yin fleed; the glib yin
Intilled the pailace.

The quick person hid;
The strong one fled; the glib one
Entered the palace.

OLD MAD PROF'S ESSAYTHALAMIUM

for Erin & Lewis

> 'COME hither, child,' said the old Earl of Courtland to his daughter, as, in obedience to his summons, she entered his study; 'Come hither, I say; I wish to have some serious conversation with you: so dismiss your dogs, shut the door, and sit down here.'
>
> Susan Ferrier, *Marriage* (1818), opening sentence of Chapter 1

TWO months back, as I may have mentioned, I searched for Strehlow's *Songs of Central Australia*, but couldn't find a copy for sale online anywhere in the world. Probably, that's as it ought to be: you shouldn't be able to buy anyone's spirit country. You can't just appropriate souls. I'd heard about Strehlow from Les Murray nearly forty years ago & read a few of Strehlow's translations of Aboriginal l&-love songs of Central Australia in two of Murray's anthologies. Sorry all this sounds so locked-in-the-library/show-offy/ egotistically PhD-ish, but, please, bear with me. I've spent ages marinated in over-endogamous essays written by the staff-student SAS of academic essayese: its parentheses barnacle your mind. Plus, I've (co-)edited anthologies too [the word 'anthology' comes from Greek *anthos* (flower) & *logos* (word), btw]. So it's become second nature to pinch red, red roses from other people's gardens, especially when flower-arranging a grade-A wedding bouquet. Think of this as a h&fasting, ancestral singalong: a wandery, welcome-to-the-family annotated wedding-speech-cum-auld-lang-syne-ceilidh-corroboree. It's in lecture-room prose & you'll just have to find any poetry in it for yourself. (When Lewis, was young, btw, he & I had lunch once (?salmon) with the poet Murray in a Thai restaurant in St &rews & we talked a lot about fish – which were then Lewis's obsession – especially about cichlids in Lake Tanganyika we'd seen on TV. Les later sent L a postcard of Oz tropical fish which stayed for years blu-tacked on his bedroom wall along with salt-water & fresh-water fish posters & pics from all over the world). Have I left anything out? I plan to add footnotes & a 'Further Reading' list later.

Great Ganges, & immortall Euphrates, *[this is weddingy stuff in Spenser's* Faerie Qveene*]*
  Deep Indus, & Mae&er intricate,
  Slow Peneus, & tempestuous Phasides, *[need to google these rivers & some others!]*
  Swift Rhene, & Alpheus still immaculate:
  Coraxes, feared for *great* Cyrus fate; *[fearèd]*
  Tybris, renowned for the Romaines fame, *[you need to pronounce it as 'renownèd']*
  Rich Oranochy, though but knowen late; *[must be the Orinoco, though it sounds Gaelic!]*
  & that huge Riuer, which doth beare his name
Of warlike Amazons, which doe possesse the same. *[wow! – Spenser & the River Amazon]*

BOTH the Dee & the Don, the fished, farmed Tweedledee & -dum of rivers me&dering through the lovely *Alice in Wonderl&* of Aberdeenshire (granitic, salmon-rich, &, says Tacitus' *Agricola*, emblematic of freedom-fighting), are beautiful, but (because he grew up there) my father, Nelson, thought the Don the lovelier, & loved Alford (on Donside), where his own dad (dead before I was born), was minister at the West Kirk with the Leochel-Cushnie Burn gushing through its glebe at Annfield (now 'Mansefield') towards the Don as family & congregation bowed their heads to pray 'Our Father', & found old metal communion tokens used by the flock dated as far back as 'Alford 1708', & my dad-to-be's sister Jean cooked because their mother, Agnes (my gran), was blind, though she could knit & run her h&s over your face & saw her children's futures much further than they could– Nelson, John, & Jean – as they stravaiged across the fields, or rode black Shetl& ponies, maybe past the Battle of Alford site, or to Tullynessle, or towards the pink tower-house at Craigievar – part-built while the poet Edmund

Spenser still walked, ran, danced, rode, & sailed. [See also wedding-speech PowerPoint 2. Check names & dates.]

Along the shoare of silver streaming *Themmes*, *[not quite internet streaming!]*
Whose rutty Bancke, the which his River hemmes, *[like hems on a wedding dress]*
Was paynted all with variable flowers, *[cp* 'variables' *in computing?]*
& all the meads adornd with daintie gemmes, *[meadows, but maybe also 'maids'?]*
Fit to decke maydens bowres,
& crowne their Paramours,
Agaynst the Brydale day, which is not long:
Sweete *Themmes* runne softly, till I end my Song. *[odd how 'Themmes' is 'T' + 'hemmes']*

A COUPLE more things (*Sermon*): when you fall in love you see things in the other person no one else can see. It's why one person can be another person's Lourdes. You can sense the miracle happening in Sappho's poems, the 'Song of Songs', *Pride & Prejudice* or *Persuasion*: it stitches you together, like a seam linking two bodies, minds, souls. It's a love-pun joining textiles, tech styles – & text isles (like the word *Lewis* or the word *Erin* printed on an isl& on a map). It's the core place you live in, though you live in other places too. Some – Craigievar / Dyce / Iona / Aboyne / East Kilbride / Haddo House / St &rews / Glasgow / Edinburgh / Shettleston / Derry / Central Australia – are on maps, but others are not . . . Now, what was the other thing? Hang on: I may have skipped a page, &, in the context of endogamy/exogamy, I want now to call up a screenshot . . .

The first, the gentle Shure that making way *[more googling needed, &/or local nous]*
By sweet Clonnell, adorns rich Waterford;
The next, the stubborne Newre, whose waters gray
By faire Kilkenny & Rosseponte boord,

The third, the goodly Barow, which doth hoard
Great heapes of Salmons in his deepe bosome:
All which long sundred, doe at last accord
To ioyne in one, ere to the sea they come,
So flowing all from one, all one at last become.

TWO secs . . . Oh yes, the only poetry my father, Nelson (not bookish, but a lover of the soil & gardening), could recite was the Aberdeenshire Doric of Murray ([Charles] b. Alford, 1864; buried, Alford, 1941), the only poet my young dad had ever seen in the flesh – until once, much later, he sat up drinking Glenmorangie with Murray (Les) who was a great eco-poet before that term was much used & who was sort of kin to Murray of the *OED* (he claimed), though not to Charles, yarning about Australia & Scotl& & who wasn't then well. Well, anyway, Murray from Alford (a white imperialist [as was Edmund Spenser] who spent much of his life in South Africa long before the days of Nelson M&ela, & whose funeral my gr&father oversaw when it looked as if we'd lose World War II) was always called 'Hamewith' after his best-known poem & book & you still see Scottish houses called 'Hamewith', & houses elsewhere – even in the antholothropologists Spencer [Baldwin Spencer not Edmund Spenser] & Gillen's Australia & in Scotl& & in Irel& & Engl& & Canada & America & Africa – because 'hamewith' is Doric for 'homewards': 'Hamewith – the road that's never dreary,/ Back where the heart is a' the time.' [add page reference] Not in the original copy of the book my dad had as a boy, but in the Aberdeen Uni Press edition my mother Betty inscribed on dad's 65th (21 October 1979) she has written in her Greenock Academy italic script 'To Nelson with love' & the date of his birthday (Trafalgar Day, 21 October), & the poem 'Hamewith' is printed opposite the poet's own printed dedication '*To my wife*'.

Most glorious Lord of lyfe, that on this day, *[This form is called a Spenserian sonnet]*
Didst make thy triumph ouer death & sin: *[It's from Spenser's sequence, 'Amoretti']*

& hauing harrowd hell, didst bring away
captuity thence captiue vs to win:
This ioyous day, deare Lord, with ioy begin,
& grant that we for whom thou diddest dye
being with thy deare blood clene washt from sin,
may liue for euer in felicity.
& that thy loue we weighing worthily,
may likewise loue thee for the same againe:
& for thy sake that all lyke deare didst buy,
with loue may one another entertayne.
So let vs loue, dear loue, lyke as we ought,
loue is the lesson which the Lord vs taught. *[It fairly takes the biscuit!]*

BOTH World Wars caught my dad. Born about a month after the Great War kicked off, he fought as a Scots Guards Lance-Corporal with a tank battalion in World War II, but he talked far more about Alford: salmon left as a poacher's gift on the manse doorstep; his own dad feeding a pony from a Heinz '57 Varieties' cardboard box; climbing Bennachie; Bogieshalloch, Tombrake [check sp.], Tarl&. Wherever he was, his spirit country was Strathdon. When I look at the map in Patrick Forbes's *6th Guards Tank Brigade: The Story of Guardsmen in Churchill Tanks* (London: Sampson, Low, Marston & Co., no date), I see not just where Nelson was – from Arromanches & Caumont, then through Bayeux & difficult Norm&y, then all over body-strewn Operation Market Garden sites near Tilburg & Nijmegen, then north-east to Cologne & north to Lübeck & Kiel (every so often there's a red dot for 'Places Liberated' & every so often a red square for 'Major Engagements') – but I see also embossed with a domestic embosser on the book's dedication page is the pale but wholly legible address, THE MANSE, ALFORD, ABERDEENSHIRE. My dad said almost nothing about those 'Major Engagements' (I think now he may have suffered PTSD), but he loved to tell how, after the war, he met my mother, Miss E. (Betty) M. MacLean, in London; & she loved to tell how, when he first approached her when she came to work as a teller in the Bank of Scotl&, Regent Street, where he too was a teller, he thoughtfully showed her where she could hang her hat. They met for a first date (a concert) on the steps of St Martin in the Fields, &, not so long afterwards, became engaged. As another poet (Robert Fergusson [?]) says, 'Best to be blyth'. [Alice, please would you be willing to look over this essaythalamium? I know there should be more in it about us.]

Ring ye the bells, ye yong men of the towne, *[young]*
& leaue your wonted labors for this day:
This day is holy; doe ye write it downe,
That ye for euer it remember may.
This day the sunne is in his chiefest hight,
With Barnaby the bright, *[haven't a clue!]*
From whence declining daily by degrees,
He somewhat loseth of his heat & light,
When once the Crab behind his back he sees, *[stuff about stars/ constellations]*
But for this time it ill ordained was,
To chose the longest day in all the yeare, *[joke about midsummer weddings]*
& shortest night, when longest fitter weare:
Yet neuer day so long, but late would passe.
Ring ye the bells, to make it weare away,
& bonefiers make all day, *[bonfires]*
& daunce about them, & about them sing: *[a sort of Spenserian corroboree or ceilidh]*
that all the woods may answer, & your echo ring.

A COUPLE develop their own language – touch, glances, phrases, pictures, flowers – almost like a code with a whole glossary (*aivrins* – cloudberry; *bucht* – a cattle-fold; *doonsitting* – a drinking bout; or, a settlement in marriage). Like DNA, or computer code or those long strings of 'entangled life' Merlin Sheldrake writes about in his book on fungi, it seems wandered, wandering, full of redundant bits, str&s of life gone walkabout or daft stuff from dreams that show us how to love each other & the planet. But you have to trust & nurture & search that code, that kith & kin dream-place because, in a strange way it is both where you live & life itself & will lead you home (hamewith). It'll help you, too, find whoever is your home. Sometimes you have to be like a nurse nursing a patient. You need to be patient, or even *a* patient. You need to find the place where therapy & art meet. Aristophanes (to whom that *When Harry Met Sally* stuff about finding 'The One' is attributed) knew this, as did our endo-exogamous ancestors, & poets like Spenser & Murray too. The code will misfire, & get tangled up. It's an embroidery where the sampler's front (imagine an elaborate, needle-worked HOME SWEET HOME) is clear, but the back's a dense Australian bush of threads, a messy meshed wiring without which the front couldn't be read. But the code still has its own wisdom, a kind of *nous* that's forever young. Sometimes you have to search & search & search; & in the background I can hear Neil Young singing 'Forever Young.'

Lyke as a huntsman after weary chace, *[another from 'Amoretti', with some punning]*
seeing the game from him escapt away, *[the sexual politics of 'game' are awkward, but this involves*
sits downe to rest him in some shady place, *a bit of Renaissance gaming]*
with panting hounds beguiled of their pray: *[pronounced here 'beguilèd'] [prey]*
So after long pursuit & vaine assay, *['assay' = 'essay' in the old sense of an 'attempt']*
when I all weary had the chace forsook,
the gentle deare returnd the self-same way, *[a huntsman's pun on 'deer' & 'dear']*
thinking to quench her thirst at the next brooke.
There she beholding me with mylder looke,
sought not to fly, but fearlesse still did bide:
till I in h& her yet halfe trembling tooke,
& with her owne goodwill hir fyrmely tyde.
Strange thing me seemed to see a beast so wyld,
So goodly wonne with her owne will beguyld. *[pronounced here 'beguiled'(!)]*

TWO peas in a pod, two rivers, Dee & Don, two chopsticks, two-by-two into Noah's Ark, tea for two, two to tango, two to dance those Jane Austen-y, Susan Ferrier-ish dances – often with others in Regency lines & reels & rings – but ultimately, however many, we come back, as I was saying above, to two: two silhouettes on a wedding website or two great rivers. As a numeral, *2* looks like a swan, & as a roman **II** it looks like you & me, Alice, or like our parents, or an engaged couple in our children's generation, a couple maybe st&ing front-to-front, about to bow, then dance. A good marriage holds many puns, including still-to-be-discovered puns (see Murray). Around the time we got engaged, Alice & I (aka, back then, the White Rabbit) discovered we had been born in the same hospital. It was as if, in hyper-*When Harry Met Sally*-style, we'd been searching for each other since before we had words. & now, when you, Erin, have arranged online with an Aberdeenshire photographer to have engagement photographs taken at Craigievar, did you know at some level that the gr&father of the man you are marrying had grown up only about five miles north of there, in Alford? Every incident has to find its co-incident, & most people long to find the one that's hers or his – some search & search forever. Now, then, oh yes, where was I? Something, maybe, about texting, texts, & ampers&s?

GLOSSE. *[This prose is from Spenser's glossary on his poem about the month of June]*

> Paradise) A Paradise in Greeke signifieth a Garden of pleasure, or place of delights. So he compareth the soile, wherin Hobbinol *[a shepherd]* made his abode, to that earthly Paradise, in scripture called Eden; wherein Adam in his first creation was placed. Which of the most learned is thought to be in Mesopotamia, the most fertile & pleasaunte country in the world (as may appeare by Diodorus Syculus *[google him]* description of it, in the hystorie of Alex&ers conquest thereof) lying between the two famous Ryvers (which are sayd in scripture to flowe out of Paradise) Tygris & Euphrates, whereof it is so denominate. *[in other words, 'Mesopotamia' means the l& between two rivers]*

BOTH the terms 'engagement' & 'major engagement' can mean battle. But you have to believe their predominant meaning is love. & when you are driving home whether between the Dee & the Don, or anywhere else, & your man is cooking in the kitchen – maybe salmon jalfrezi or maybe a Thai fish curry – after a long day of coding & decoding folk, showing what it means to follow ever-lengthening threads, you might like to remember 'Hamewith' & your engagement pictures at Craigievar. & when you peer at those pictures & at your wedding album in years to come you might wonder just who is in them. Is it you & your husb&, or is it some other man, young & vulnerable in not a pea-coat but a big-lapelled, military-looking coat? Is Craigievar the place of Spenser's day [the place of *The Faerie Quine*] or of Disney (at the start of the title sequence of *Cinderella*), a star flickering high on dreamtime battlements, or maybe of folk not yet born & who have not yet danced or read any of the books in the lovely library at Haddo House, but who one day, en route to a ball / ceilidh / corroboree, will search & find a copy of Strehlow's *Songs of Central Australia*, or Austen, or Ferrier, or Spenser's poems, or the poets Murray, or a copy of *Hamewith*, & find inside the two words 'With love' & underst& them, & the meaning of the library, & life's one lasting meaning, which is just, after all, one word.

Rivers, flow softly while I end my song.

FROM BOOK V OF THE GREEK ANTHOLOGY

84

As a deep pink rose
I feel your hand pulling me
Between your warm breasts.

91

This perfume is yours
Not as a gift but because
You perfume perfume.

128

We are breast-to-breast,
Lip to lip, now only one
Lit candle sees us.

295

Wineglass, touch her wet
Lips – I'd feel no jealousy
If your luck was mine.

FOREST BATHING

The Latin *liber*
Means *book* or *free*, and the root
Of *book* means *beech wood*.

Among foliage,
Nested in thickets of staves,
Perch the words of songs.

TRUELOVE

I love you because,
Unfazed, you're a bone china
Teacup in a storm.

ACKNOWLEDGEMENTS

[illegible] of these poems [illegible] appeared in [illegible] [illegible] [illegible] Samsara [illegible] [illegible] [illegible] [illegible] [illegible] in my collaboration with the [illegible] [illegible] [illegible] 2019 [illegible] the [illegible] [illegible] [illegible] [illegible] [illegible] [illegible] with [illegible] [illegible] was exhibited at the [illegible] [illegible] [illegible] by the [illegible] [illegible].

[illegible] [illegible] to my [illegible] [illegible] [illegible] [illegible] [illegible] [illegible] [illegible] [illegible] poems [illegible] [illegible] [illegible] [illegible] [illegible] [illegible] and [illegible] [illegible] [illegible] [illegible].

ACKNOWLEDGEMENTS

Some of these poems have appeared in *Essays in Criticism, London Review of Books*, *Poetry London*, and the *Scotsman*. The three versions of Song Dynasty Chinese poems appeared in my collaboration with the photographer Norman McBeath, *Strath* (Easel Press, 2019), and earlier versions of some of the 'Old World Emblems' appeared as part of my book *Classical Texts* (Kettillonia, 2021) and as part of *Gone Viral*, a suite of work made in collaboration with the artist Arthur Watson which was exhibited at the Royal Scottish Academy in 2022 and published by the artist as an artist's book.

I owe a debt to my friend the Mexican poet Pedro Serrano, who asked me some years ago if I had any poems about animals. Well, now I have. Thanks are due, too, to Alice Crawford and David Kinloch for reading and commenting on drafts.